The Orange Grove

and Other Stories

Rosanne Keller

SIGNAL HILL™
PUBLICATIONS

ATTENTION READERS: We would like to hear what you think about our books. Please send your comments or suggestions to:

Signal Hill Publications
P.O. Box 131
Syracuse, NY 13210-0131

SIGNAL HILL™

PUBLICATIONS

ISBN 0-88336-558-8

Copyright © 1992
Signal Hill Publications
A publishing imprint of Laubach Literacy International
Box 131, Syracuse, New York 13210-0131

Printed in the United States of America

Illustrated by Cheri Bladholm

9 8 7 6 5 4 3

The
Orange
Grove
and Other Stories

Table of Contents

The
Orange
Grove

"The Answer Is No!"

"But, Papá, I love him!" cries Rosa. "I can't live without him!"

"You will not marry a migrant worker!" says José. He is speaking Spanish. His face is like stone. "That is my last word. We will not discuss this again!"

"But, Papá, *you* are a migrant worker," Rosa says. She touches his arm. "We are all migrant workers."

"The answer is no!" José says. His voice is loud and rough. He pulls his arm away from Rosa's hand. He looks angry. But his heart is breaking.

Rosa runs out the door crying.

José knows the young man Rosa says she can't live without. His name is Manuel Hernández. He is a hard worker. José has worked with him many times.

José has seen Manuel look at Rosa. He has seen her smile back. Their eyes are full of love.

But Manuel is a migrant worker like me, José thinks. I want more for my Rosa.

José looks out at the grove where they pick oranges. He sees the row of old shacks where the workers live. There are broken windows and cracked doors. We will move on from here, he thinks. Who knows where we will live next?

"Why are you so hard on her?" asks Dolores.

José looks at his wife. Dolores is on her knees in the dirt in front of their shack. She puts a piece of sheet iron across the fire. She is cooking tortillas to sell to other workers. He watches her kneeling there by the smoky fire. She has never owned a stove.

"Manuel has never gone to school," José says. "He cannot speak English. He will always be a field-worker. He will never do better than the fields and orange groves."

"But our Rosa will," he says. He looks at his daughter sitting under an orange tree. She is still crying. "She will have a better life. She will not marry a man who works in the fields."

José leans against the door of the shack where they live. José and Dolores and their four children live there. José's brother Pablo and his wife and baby live in the small shack, too.

"Rosa will have a house to live in," says José. "She will marry a man who has a steady job, maybe a man who works in a factory. Her children will go to the same school every year."

"I know, José," says Dolores. "I want Rosa to be happy, too. To have a better life. But you can't stop love," she says. "It is stronger than you are."

Migrant Field-Workers

José was born in Mexico. He came to the United States through the "back door." He swam across the Río Grande. It was illegal, but he was not caught. He was glad to be in a place where he could find work. Then the best thing of all happened. He met Dolores.

José met Dolores in a tomato field. She was picking tomatoes. Her family lived in south Texas. They were Mexican-Americans.

José and Dolores fell in love. When they got married, José became an American citizen.

Dolores's family treated José like a son. He and Dolores lived with them.

Every spring the whole family packed up their old car and pickup truck. They traveled from one farm to another. As a family, they planted fields of vegetables.

Months later, they returned to those farms. They weeded the fields they had planted. At the end of summer, they began the harvest. They picked vegetables. Then they picked fruit.

In late fall, they traveled back to the citrus groves of Texas. There they picked oranges, lemons, and grapefruit.

The living conditions at the farms were usually bad. Dirty shacks with no windows to keep bugs out. No running water. Sometimes the family even lived in tents.

José and Dolores had four children. When the children were old enough, they worked, too. Rosa began picking strawberries when she was seven years old. She only went to school once in a while.

That has always made José feel sad.

Sunday Morning

The next morning, José wakes up late. He hears Rosa singing outside. It is a sad song.

José crawls out of the hard bed he built of boards. Dolores is still sleeping.

It is cool outside in the orange grove. José sees Rosa washing her hair in a bucket.

It is Sunday. They do not have to work on Sundays. Maybe José's brother Pablo will play his guitar later. The children can play with the ball they found. It will be a fine day, José thinks.

José leans back against the wall of the shack. The wood is warm on his back.

Dolores comes out, yawning. She and Rosa start cooking. José can smell the Mexican food he loves. Rosa starts singing again. This time she sings a happier song.

Rosa has always loved to sing. When she was little, she used to sing the family to sleep. José smiles and thinks about when Rosa was a little girl.

He closes his eyes. José remembers many nights in shacks like this one. Everyone would be in bed, tired from the back-breaking work in the fields. Sometimes it was windy or rainy outside. But they felt safe because they were together. José loved to hear his family breathing in the dark as they slept. He could feel their warmth.

"Sing us a song, Rosa," he often said. And Rosa sang. Her clear, young voice filled the room. José remembers falling asleep thinking how good life was.

"Are you going to fall asleep there?" Dolores asks.

José opens his eyes. He smiles at Dolores. The food smells good. The boys are chasing each other around the orange trees. Rosa is playing with Pablo's baby.

We live a hard life, José thinks. But it's a good life.

Working the Land

It is the next Saturday evening. José and his family have been picking oranges all day. José is tired. He's nervous, too. He paces back and forth in front of his shack. He is waiting for Manuel.

Manuel has asked José to go for a drive with him. He wants to talk with José alone.

José knows what this is about. Manuel is going to ask to marry Rosa. José will tell him he can't.

Manuel's rusty old pickup truck comes down the road. It stops in front of José. Manuel gets out. One door is tied closed with rope. Manuel unties it for José to get in.

Then Manuel drives out on the highway. At first, he and José don't talk. Manuel turns off on a dirt road. He stops at an orange grove.

"This is where I worked today," he says. "I picked more oranges than anyone else."

"Are you proud of that?" asks José.

"Yes," says Manuel.

"Well," says José in a mocking voice. "I guess that makes you the best orange picker around." He says "orange picker" as if he is saying a dirty word.

Manuel doesn't seem to notice that José is making fun of him.

"A man from the packing company came by today," says Manuel. "He talked to the owner of this grove."

"What did they talk about?" asks José.

"They want me and two others to work at the packing company," answers Manuel. "They need men who will work hard."

"That sounds like steady work," José says. He turns and looks at Manuel. "What did you say?"

Manuel doesn't answer right away. He takes a deep breath. Then he says, "I said 'no.'"

"Are you crazy?" José shouts. "I thought you were going to beg me to let you marry Rosa." He stares hard at Manuel. "Now you tell me you turned down a real job?"

"I don't beg," says Manuel quietly. "But I do want to tell you what you already know. I love your daughter. I want to marry her."

"You know I do not want her to marry you. I don't want her to spend her life in the fields," says José. "She deserves a better life than that."

"Do you think she has been unhappy with her life?" asks Manuel. "Did you ever ask her? She says she has had a good life. She tells me about it. Traveling with the whole family. Sleeping in one room. Singing songs and telling stories."

"There have been hard times, too," says José. "Does she tell you about those?"

"Yes," says Manuel. "She tells me that sometimes she slept on dirt floors. And ate cold beans. She tells me about being cold working out in the rain. And being hot out in the sun."

Manuel picks up an orange lying on the front seat. "She remembers working bent over all day," he says. "She says that many times she thought her back would break."

Manuel turns and looks at José. "But she says she does not mind hard work." Manuel takes another deep breath. "Neither do I."

"But," says José, "if you had a steady job, you could live in a house. You could send your kids to school."

"Yes," says Manuel. "That may be true. I could work inside a building with no windows all day. Rosa could clean other people's houses. Our children would hardly see us."

Manuel looks out at the orange grove. "Families work together here."

Manuel holds out his rough hands. "I am a farm worker," he says. "Everyone in my family has worked on the land. I can't work in a place with no windows. I like planting seeds and watching them grow. I like seeing plants blossom." He smiles. "I love the harvest. I enjoy knowing people will eat the fruits and vegetables I pick."

The door of the truck creaks as Manuel opens it. He gets out and walks to the edge of the field.

José unties his door and gets out, too.

"Look at this orange grove," Manuel says. "I work here every day. I love it. I don't care if it's hot, or cold, or even raining. I like the smell of the air." He turns to José. "I worked in a building for a while. Inside all day. I didn't like it."

José watches the sun going down over the trees. He remembers times when he had jobs inside buildings. He hated them.

Manuel goes on talking. "I am happy when I come to the fields and groves. I think it is important work."

"But what about your future?" asks José. "It is a hard life being a migrant worker. You know that."

"I know," says Manuel. "But I like working with my family. I like working with my friends. When we are all in a field or a grove together, it is good. It feels . . ." He lifts his shoulders. "It feels like we are all a part of something bigger than ourselves. Do you ever feel like that?"

José sighs. He nods his head. "Yes," he says. "I know what you are talking about."

"I know Rosa loves me," says Manuel. "She respects me for being a field-worker." He looks at José. "This may surprise you. There is

another man she loves and respects even more."

José jerks his head around. "Who?" he asks.

"You," answers Manuel softly. He points at the orange grove. "The man who taught her to value this."

José turns away and goes back to the truck. He does not want Manuel to see his tears. "Take me home now," he says.

They don't talk on the drive back. When they pull up to the shack, José reaches over. He presses the horn on the truck. He honks it until everyone comes running.

"I have something to tell you," José shouts. He unties the rope and gets out of the truck. He waits until everyone is quiet. Then he smiles at Rosa.

"Start cooking and get out the guitar," José says in a proud voice. "Let's celebrate! We are going to have a wedding!"

The
Granny
Group

"Growing Old Is Awful!"

Martina looks into her closet. Which dress should she wear? Which shoes? It is so hard to choose. Maybe she should get her glasses.

Martina looks around. Now where are her glasses? She puts her hand to her mouth. Good. She has remembered her teeth. Martina reaches down for her shoes and groans.

Growing old is so hard. You forget things. Your joints ache. You have to depend on other people for so many things.

"Growing old is awful!" Martina says out loud. "Now where did I put my glasses?"

"Are you talking to me or to yourself?" shouts Felipe. He speaks in Spanish. Felipe is Martina's grandson. He is waiting for her in the living room.

"I'm talking to myself!" Martina says. "But I don't hear any answers."

Felipe laughs. Martina loves to make him laugh.

Martina finds her glasses on a chair. "It's lucky I didn't sit on them," she says. She is talking to herself again.

Martina lives with her daughter Paz in Los Angeles. Felipe is the last child still at home. He is in high school. School is out now for the summer.

Martina spends three hours a day at the Senior Center. She eats lunch at the center. Felipe drives her there.

Paz found out about the Senior Center three years ago. She told Martina, "It's just for senior citizens. Anyone over age 65 can go there. You can take classes there." It was perfect for Martina. She was 67 years old then.

Martina has already taken weaving and painting classes. She likes to read. She often uses the library at the center.

Martina has made many friends at the Senior Center. There is only one thing she doesn't like. Everyone who goes there is her age . . . or older!

But most of the people who work there are young and full of energy. Martina's favorite staff person is Meg. Meg is about 30 years old. She is the mother of adorable young twins. Meg is in charge of exercise and games. She works every morning. She is so friendly that everyone loves her.

"Come on, Grandmother," calls Felipe. "Let's go. I'm meeting the guys at the mall. I don't want to be late."

Martina sighs. Felipe wants to be with his friends all the time. Young people are always in a hurry, Martina thinks.

Martina hopes her friend Kate will come today. Kate is fun. She is always doing something. Kate takes classes in watercolor painting at the Senior Center. She also takes classes in French cooking. She is even part of the jazz dance group. Meg teaches the class. Kate calls it "slow jazz for old ladies."

But not everyone at the Senior Center takes the classes. Many people just come and sit. They seem to be waiting. What are they waiting for? Martina doesn't like to think about it.

When Martina comes into the living room, Felipe asks, "Why do you get so dressed up? You aren't going to a wedding. It's only lunch."

Martina looks at the floor. She knows he is right. What is she getting all dressed up for? For lunch with those tired, gray-haired old people.

And I'm just another one of them, Martina thinks. Just an old Mexican woman in a strange new world.

All at once Martina feels her age. It hangs on her like a heavy weight. Growing old is so hard, she thinks again.

Lunch at the Senior Center

Martina walks into the Senior Center dining room. It is very noisy. There are people at every table. She looks around for her friend Kate.

She sees Kate across the room. "Over here, Martina," Kate shouts. She is waving both hands. "I saved you a seat."

Sitting at the table with Kate is Payson. Payson is Chinese. Martina has known her for years. They are neighbors.

"Don't you look nice," says Kate. Then she smiles. "But don't we all? Let's go get our lunch."

Kate looks around at all the people. "I painted a picture of this room in class once," she says.

"Oh?" says Martina. "Where is the painting?"

"It's at home. I paint so many pictures. And for what? I put them on my walls." Kate smiles sadly. "But I live alone, you know. I am the only person who ever sees them."

"That's all right if you enjoy painting them," says Martina.

"No, just painting them is not enough," says Kate. "You need to do paintings for other people." She looks at Martina and Payson sadly. "I don't have anyone to paint them for."

Payson speaks for the first time. "I have people to do things for. I live with my son and his wife and my four grandchildren. But they are not interested in what I do. They want to be like other Americans. They think this means giving up all the old ways."

Payson leans forward. "But I want them to be proud to be Chinese. I want to tell them about China. They listen politely, but they do not hear. They do not have time for an old Chinese grandmother."

"It's a shame," Kate says. "Is this what getting old means? Not being needed by anyone?"

"That is how I often feel," says Payson. Then she brightens. "Wouldn't it be nice to have something to wake up for each day? Something to do?"

"Yes," says Martina. "I'd like to get out more and *do* things. But I'm afraid to go out. It's not safe on the streets where we live. I have no place to go except here." Martina sighs. "Sometimes I feel so useless."

Payson looks at Martina and then at Kate. "What good is it to grow old and wise? What good is it if no one wants your wisdom?"

Meg's Problem

"Here comes Meg," says Martina. "She is one young person who listens to us."

"What would we do without her?" says Kate. "Meg is the one who gets us moving. She gets us old birds on our feet to exercise."

"Hello, ladies," says Meg. Meg has worked at the Senior Center since Martina joined. She can get almost anyone to exercise.

People might complain. They might say they are too tired or too old. But they will exercise for Meg.

Meg looks so young to Martina. Her hair is short. Her big gold earrings shine against her dark skin. She's very pretty.

"How are you all doing?" Meg asks.

"We were just talking about that," says Payson.

"We were also talking about you," says Kate. "We don't know what we'd do without you." Kate reaches out and touches Meg's hand. "How are your little twins? Didn't they just have a birthday?"

"Yes," says Meg. "Todd and Annie are two years old now."

Then Meg stops smiling. "Ladies, I have some bad news," she says. "I have to quit working here."

"Oh, no," says Kate.

"But why?" asks Payson.

Martina's heart feels like a stone.

"I leave the twins at a very nice day-care center nearby," says Meg, "but it's closing. I can't leave them there anymore. I don't want to quit this job. But my children come first." She looks out the window. Her eyes look very sad.

Then she says softly, "I love it here. This job is perfect for me. I only work in the mornings. I can spend the afternoons with Todd and Annie. The day-care center is good for them. They get to know other people while I work. I think children need that."

"Can't you find another place for them?" asks Martina. "Even a baby-sitter?"

"I've looked," says Meg. "I just can't find a place I feel good about."

Then Meg smiles. "I'm sorry. That's enough about my problems," she says. "Well, have a nice lunch, ladies." She turns away quickly. But they see her wipe away a tear.

Grannies to the Rescue

"Oh, no. What can we do?" asks Payson.

"What will we do? We are losing someone we depend on. We need Meg," says Martina.

"You did not understand me," says Payson. "I said, 'What *can* we do?' Why don't *we* do something? We may feel useless. But we are not helpless."

"We can't teach the exercise classes," says Kate.

"But we could take care of Meg's children," says Payson. "Who could do it better than wise grandmothers like us?"

"Where would we take care of them?" asks Martina.

"Hmmm, that is a problem," says Payson. She shakes her head. "Maybe it is not possible."

They all think for a few moments. "I know," says Kate. "We can keep the children at my house. I only live one block from here."

"What a good idea," says Payson. She smiles and nods. "We can start a day-care center of our own."

Kate laughs. "Our own day-care center," she says. "We could call it 'The Granny Group.'"

But Martina looks worried. "Two little children would be a handful," she says. "I wouldn't want to be alone with them. Something might happen."

"We could take turns watching the children," says Kate. "Two of us at a time. We could take turns coming to the Senior Center, too. After all, it's only the mornings. I wonder if Meg's twins will like my paintings," Kate says.

"You could teach them to paint," says Martina. "This would be so much fun. Let's go talk to Meg."

Meg is just leaving the office. She looks surprised when the three women come in. She listens to what they have to say. Then her look of surprise becomes a smile of joy.

"That's a wonderful idea," she says. "I know you ladies well. I can't think of anyone I trust more. This is great!"

"Would we have to have a permit?" asks Kate. "Or a license?"

"I don't think so," says Meg. "Not for only two children. I'll find out. But I'm almost sure there is no problem."

"In that case, bring them over tomorrow," says Kate. "The Granny Group is open for business!"

The Granny Group

It is a month later. Payson is eating lunch at the Senior Center. Meg sees her. "Hello," she says. "I see you've got a day off from the kids."

"Today is Kate and Martina's turn," says Payson. "Kate is teaching the children to finger paint."

"This is perfect for me," Meg says. "I love having the children nearby." She smiles at Payson. "And they love all their 'grannies.'"

"Two other women here have asked if they can help," Payson says. "And you know the nurse who comes here on Wednesday mornings?"

Meg nods.

"She wants us to watch her little boy, too," says Payson.

"I know," says Meg. "I told her about the Granny Group. Would you grannies like another child? Would it be too much?"

"We have already said yes," says Payson. She smiles. "Martina tells me that your Todd is speaking Spanish. He speaks Spanish as well as he speaks English. That is what she says."

"That is not saying much," Meg laughs. "He doesn't know a lot of English."

They laugh. Then Payson says, "And Annie listens to all my stories about China. Even when I tell them in Chinese."

Stranger at the Door

Stranger at the Door

Desta opens the curtain. She looks out at the street. It is getting dark.

Where is Makeda, Desta wonders? Why is she so late?

Desta worries about her daughter, Makeda. Makeda is only 18 years old. She works in a clothing factory on the other side of New York City. After work she goes to an English class. She rides the subway home each night. Desta is afraid that the streets are not safe after dark.

Desta sighs. She looks around the small apartment. She and Makeda live here with Desta's mother, Gennet.

The living room is filled with things from Ethiopia. There are carvings of black wood and red curtains with gold fringes. For Desta, this room is a small Ethiopia.

There are also baskets of many colors.
Desta and her mother weave them. Then they
sell them to flower shops. When Desta thinks
of Ethiopia, she feels sad. She likes living in
America. But this does not stop her from
being homesick.

Where could Makeda be? Desta walks back
and forth. She looks around the room. Her old
mother is sitting on the floor. She always sat on
the floor in Ethiopia. She is weaving a basket.

This apartment is Gennet's world now, Desta thinks. Then she goes to the window. But it is not Makeda's world. Makeda must make her own way out in the world. What will become of Makeda in this strange land? In this strange land where the Ethiopian ways are not important?

Desta sighs. She looks out the window again. All she sees is a group of young men standing under the streetlight. Where can Makeda be?

Running Home

At last, Desta sees her daughter coming up the street. Makeda is running.

Desta is relieved. She feels proud, as always, when she sees Makeda. The young men watch as Makeda runs by.

Makeda is six feet tall, slim, and graceful. She moves like a willow tree blowing in the wind. Her face is like a perfectly made wood carving. Even in Ethiopia people stopped to stare at her.

"She's coming," says Desta to her mother. She watches Makeda run up the sidewalk.

I named her well, Desta thinks. Makeda, the name of a great queen in Ethiopia. A queen the whole world knows as the Queen of Sheba.

Makeda opens the door and comes in quickly. She looks afraid. She is out of breath.

"What is wrong?" asks Desta.

"A man is following me," says Makeda. "He spoke to me on the subway."

"What man?" Desta asks.

"I don't know him," says Makeda. "But I've seen him before. He is always watching me."

"What did he say, Makeda?" Desta is worried.

"I can't understand him," says Makeda. "He talks too fast. It was something about photos. He wants to take my picture." She takes a card out of her pocket. "He gave me this."

"What does it say?" asks Desta.

"It is a name and address," says Makeda.

"What does this man look like?" Desta wants to know.

Makeda thinks. "He is not old. He has blond hair combed back. He wears a tie." She looks at her mother. "He acts friendly. Too friendly. He keeps trying to talk to me."

"Does he talk to other people?" Desta asks.

"Yes. I've seen him talk to another woman," Makeda says. "She took his card too." Makeda runs to the window. "I just hope he didn't see where I went."

Makeda looks very worried. Desta is afraid. She is afraid of this man who bothers young women. She is afraid for her beautiful daughter.

The Visitor

Makeda pulls back the curtain. "Oh, no," she cries. "He did see. He's coming into the building."

"This is not good," old Gennet says. Her fingers move quickly, weaving the basket.

Just then the doorbell rings.

Desta feels her heart beating. She goes to the door. But she does not open it.

"Go away," she shouts. She forgets to speak English.

The man is talking.

"What is he saying?" Gennet whispers from the floor. She is holding the basket tight in her hands.

"I don't know," says Desta.

"He wants to talk with me," says Makeda. "He wants to know my name."

"No!" shouts Desta through the door. "You go away!" This time she says it in English.

But he does not go away. He keeps ringing the doorbell.

Desta is very frightened. Who is this man? Is he a mugger? Does he want to rob them? Does he want to hurt Makeda?

They can't call the police. They don't have a phone. And they can't go out for help. The man keeps talking.

Makeda goes to the door. She looks very angry. She puts on the door chain. Then she opens the door just a crack. "What do you want?" she asks.

"To talk with you," the man says.

"No!" Makeda shouts.

"Then please, just read this." Before Makeda can shut the door, he pushes an envelope through the crack. It falls to the floor.

Makeda shouts, "Go away!" She slams the door shut.

Good News?

The three women look at the envelope. They let it lie on the floor a few minutes. Desta wants to throw it out the door. Gennet wants to burn it.

Desta and Makeda know they must read it. They must find out why that man is bothering Makeda.

"Your English is good," Desta says to Makeda. "See if you can translate the letter."

Makeda gets out her dictionary. She finds a pen and paper. She translates the short letter. It only takes her a few minutes.

She looks up with a smile that lights the room. "This is wonderful," she says. "This is good news!"

"What is it?" asks Desta.

"We're going to be rich!" Makeda says. Her straight, white teeth flash as she laughs. "I am going to make lots of money."

"Is that what the letter says?" Desta asks. "Is the man offering you a job?"

"Yes," laughs Makeda. "That man is a photographer. He takes photos of people. Then he helps them get jobs."

"What kind of jobs?" asks Gennet.

"Modeling jobs," Makeda says. She looks at the letter. "He says I would make a perfect model."

Desta frowns. "What kind of model?"

"For clothes," says Makeda. "It says right here. My picture could be on the cover of fashion magazines. I could be in fashion shows. I could even be a model for make-up. Or for hair styles." She laughs again.

Makeda picks up the paper she has written on. She starts to read her translation of the letter. "The fashion world is always looking for good models. Models need photos of themselves to get jobs."

She goes on. "You have won a free set of photos. All you have to do is come to our studio. We will take pictures of you. With these photos you could get a modeling job. You could model for the best fashion magazines. You could make thousands of dollars a month. The photos are free. All you pay is the sitting fee."

"What is a 'sitting fee'?" asks Desta.

"I don't know," says Makeda. "But just think. Thousands of dollars a month! And look. Here are some pictures he has taken."

She hands the photos to Desta. They are very good photos. The women in them are wearing fine clothes. All of the women are lovely.

Desta has always known that Makeda is beautiful. Perhaps this photographer will help Makeda get started in modeling. She would make a very good model.

No Promises

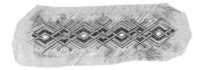

The next day is Saturday. Makeda does not have to go to work. In the afternoon, the doorbell rings again. The three women look at each other. Is it the photographer, Desta wonders? Has he come back?

Desta goes to the door. It is not the photographer. It is Makeda's English tutor, Sharon Cox. Of course, she always comes on Saturday afternoons.

"Please come in," says Desta in her best English. "It is good of you to come."

"Thank you," says Sharon. "I always enjoy coming here. You have so many beautiful things." She says hello to Makeda and Gennet.

"I have some wonderful news," Makeda says. She holds up the letter. "I am going to be a fashion model. It's in this letter."

"That's great, Makeda! Can I see the letter?" asks Sharon. She looks at the letter a long time.

"Isn't this great?" asks Makeda. "I can make a lot of money. And it will be so much fun. Maybe I'll be on TV."

"Wait a minute," says Sharon. "This letter doesn't say you will get a job. It says you *could* get a job. There is a big difference."

"What do you mean?" asks Makeda.

"I mean this doesn't promise you any jobs." She turns the letter over. "Did you know you have to pay two hundred dollars for these photos?" asks Sharon.

"Two hundred dollars?" shout Desta and Makeda at the same time. "Where does it say that?" asks Makeda.

"Right here on the back of the letter. It's written very small," says Sharon.

"But the letter says that I get the pictures free," says Makeda.

Sharon nods her head. "Yes. It does say that. But it also says that you have to pay a sitting fee. That fee is two hundred dollars."

"What is a 'sitting fee'?" asks Makeda.

"A sitting fee is what photographers charge for the film and their time in the studio," Sharon says.

She points to the letter. "This man is trying to trick you. The letter says that you'd be a perfect model. It says you'd make a lot of money. Anyone would like to make a lot of money."

"But what about the job?" asks Makeda.

"You have to go and find the job for yourself," says Sharon.

"But I don't know how to do that," says Makeda.

"I understand," says Sharon. "You see what I mean? This letter does not promise you a job. And you have to pay that sitting fee."

Makeda looks as if she is going to cry. Desta is sad to see Makeda so unhappy. Who can you trust here, Desta wonders? How can we know what to do?

Sharon looks at Makeda. "But you know, Makeda, that man is right," she says. "You could be a model."

"Do you really think so, Sharon? I'm not so sure anymore," says Makeda.

"It's time you found out," says Sharon. "I'll call a good modeling agency for you. You and I can go there together. You can ask them all the questions you want."

"Are you sure they wouldn't mind?" asks Makeda.

"Mind?" Sharon laughs. "They will think I have brought them a gift!" She puts her arm around Makeda. "You!"

Desta feels herself relax. She no longer needs to worry. Now Makeda is in good hands. Sharon will give her good advice.

Maybe one day Makeda will be a model. Maybe she will choose other work. The best thing is that she has a choice.

And now she has a friend she can trust.

Midnight
Anger

Homecoming

Paco hates to go home. Every day he feels the same. He is tired, and his job is hard. But he still hates to go home.

Paco works as a flagger on a road crew. He is helping to build a new highway around El Paso. It is hot, dusty work and very noisy. All Paco wants to do when he gets home is rest. He wants an ice-cold glass of tea and some quiet.

But does he get rest? No. He can't even have a quiet day off.

Paco can find his apartment without looking. All he has to do is follow the noise. Kids screaming, crying, laughing. And Ramona yelling at them.

Every evening, Paco walks in the door and looks around. He wants to turn and go back out. Three kids in a two-room apartment is too much. Everything is always a mess. The apartment always smells of diapers.

Midnight Madness

Paco goes home later and later every day. Sometimes he goes out with other guys from his road crew. But he doesn't even like to drink. He tries to make one drink last all evening. Anything to kill time. He hates to go home.

Paco's feelings are all mixed up. He is angry at Ramona all the time. He doesn't know why. She looks so tired. This makes Paco feel guilty. Then he gets mad.

Paco works hard. He just can't get ahead. He wishes they had a better place to live. He feels guilty again.

One Friday night, Paco gets home very late. He walks up to his door and listens. All is quiet. He takes off his shoes. Then he goes in quietly.

All he can hear is breathing. Everyone is asleep. The two little girls sleep on the couch in the living room. Ramona and the baby are in the bedroom.

Paco puts his wallet on the table. He takes off his clothes quietly and walks softly into the bedroom.

Suddenly he feels something soft under his foot. It makes a noise as he steps on it.

Oh, no, Paco thinks. I've stepped on the baby!

Paco reaches down and picks up what he stepped on. It doesn't move. He reaches for the light switch and turns it on. The baby begins to scream. The girls start crying in the next room.

Paco looks around. "Oh no," he groans. Paco feels like crying too.

The room is like a nightmare. Clothes cover the floor. Toys are everywhere. And the kids are crying!

Ramona is sitting up in bed. She's looking at Paco. Then she puts her hands over her face. Is she crying, too, Paco wonders? His heart sinks.

Ramona looks up. She does have tears in her eyes. But she is not crying. She points at Paco. She is laughing so much she can hardly talk.

Finally she says, "You look so funny standing there in your underwear. And holding that doll!" She falls back laughing.

Paco looks down. He is holding a baby doll. He is so mad, he throws it across the room. He turns and marches back into the living room. The sound of Ramona's laugh follows him.

"Fine," says Paco. "Go ahead and laugh. I'm getting out of here." He pulls on his clothes and runs to his truck.

The Diner

Paco drives around all night. Early in the morning he stops at a diner. He is so hungry he could eat anything. He sits at the counter.

"What will it be, honey?" asks the waitress. "Coffee? Breakfast?"

Paco reaches for his wallet. He wants to see how much money he has. "Oh, no," he says out loud. He has left his wallet at home on the table. He checks his pockets for change. All he has is 60 cents.

"Coffee," he says. He can hear his stomach growl. Then he remembers why. He didn't even eat dinner last night.

"Looks like you've had a rough night," says the waitress. She puts a steaming cup of coffee on the counter. She smiles at Paco. She has nice eyes.

Paco picks his coffee up. His hands are shaking. Coffee spills on the counter.

The waitress comes over with a towel. "Are you in some kind of trouble?" she asks. "If you are, you can tell Sal about it."

Paco blows on his coffee to cool it. How can he talk to this woman he doesn't even know? He wants to tell Sal that he has to go. But where would he go?

"I've heard a million stories," Sal says. She speaks with a soft Texas accent. She looks at Paco kindly. "I listen real good."

Something in Paco's chest hurts. He feels so alone.

Before he can stop himself, he starts talking. "I'm just so tired," he says.

"Then why don't you go home?" Sal asks.

"I can't go home," Paco says. "I've left my wife."

Paco thinks Sal will ask why. But instead she asks, "Do you still love her?"

"I don't know." Paco takes a sip of the hot coffee. "I just can't stand all the kids and the mess."

Paco turns away. He doesn't want this woman to see his tears. He closes his eyes.

He remembers how he felt the night
before. He remembers the messy apartment.
The crying kids. And Ramona laughing.

That is what made him so mad. She
laughed at him. In the middle of all that mess!

"How many children do you have?" Sal asks.

Paco takes a deep breath. "We have three.
The girls are two and three. The baby is 10
months," he says.

Paco waits for Sal to scold him. He thinks
she will say he has too many children. But
she says, "Do you love the children?"

"Yes, I love my children," he says. "It's just
that sometimes . . . sometimes . . ."

Sal smiles. "Tell me about your wife," she says.

"Are you sure you have time for this?" asks Paco. "You don't have to sit here and talk to me."

Sal looks around. "There is nobody here but you." She looks into Paco's eyes. "How about some breakfast?"

"I left my wallet at home," Paco says. "I don't have any money."

"There are times when money isn't important," says Sal. "What would you like? Name it. Bacon and eggs? How about some pancakes?"

Paco is so hungry his mouth waters. But he is too proud to take food. "No, thank you," he says.

Sal turns to the grill. She starts cooking anyway.

When the food is ready, Sal puts it on the counter. "I made some toast, too," she says. She pours more coffee for Paco. Then she pours herself a cup and sits down. What can Paco do but eat?

"You were talking about your wife," Sal says.

"I don't remember saying anything about Ramona," says Paco.

"But you're thinking about her." Sal nods. "What's she like?"

Paco wants to say Ramona is messy. He wants to say she yells at the kids. He wants to tell Sal how Ramona laughed at him.

"Well," he says. "I don't know. She's all right, I guess."

"So what's the problem?" asks Sal.

"She doesn't have time for me," says Paco. "Even on my day off, she does nothing but yell at the kids." There, he said it.

"Does she ever have a day off?" asks Sal.

A day off for Ramona? Paco feels as if he's been hit in the stomach. "I have never thought of that," he says. But he is thinking now. Ramona has not had a "day off" for years.

Paco remembers how tired Ramona often looks. He feels sad.

"Has Ramona complained about not having a day off?" asks Sal.

Paco stops to think. He drinks some more coffee. He remembers how he feels in that apartment. He'd go crazy if he had to stay there all day. But Ramona doesn't complain. Now Paco feels ashamed.

But he is still angry about last night. "She laughed at me," says Paco. "In the middle of all that mess and noise, she laughed."

"She laughed?" Sal shakes her head. "She must be a special woman. I think I'd cry all the time. What on earth did she laugh at?"

Paco starts to tell her. He tells of coming home late. He tells of undressing in the dark. He tells of stepping on the doll and turning on the light. He tells of everyone crying and the mess. And the laughter.

Paco doesn't look at Sal. He is too busy remembering. He tells Sal about standing there in his underwear. He tells how angry he felt. He tells about how Ramona laughed at him.

Just then Paco hears a noise. He looks over at Sal. Her hand is over her mouth. Her eyes are full of tears. Suddenly she moves her hand.

Paco can't believe it. Sal is laughing! She can't stop!

Then in his mind, Paco sees the scene. He
sees himself as Ramona saw him. Standing
there in his underwear. The kids crying. And
him holding that stupid doll.

Something rises in Paco's chest. The ache
starts to melt. He is starting to laugh.

At first it is a little laugh. Then he is roaring
with laughter.

"You must be married to a good woman,"
says Sal. She wipes her eyes. "Just think.
Ramona has to stay with those kids all the
time. She never gets out. She never gets away.
She has no time to herself." Sal looks hard at
Paco. "And still she can laugh."

Paco doesn't know what to say.

Sal goes on talking. "She doesn't have even a minute off. Much less a whole day off. And you say she doesn't complain?"

Paco has stopped laughing. He rubs his eyes.

Sal goes on talking. "She can't sit down to rest, ever. Just cook, scrub, and wipe bottoms. I bet Ramona has to clean one mess after another," she says. "No wonder everything is messy."

Paco looks at Sal. "And then I come home," he says sadly. The ache in his chest has come back.

"And you want some quiet time with Ramona," Sal says softly. "But don't forget that Ramona needs quiet time, too."

A Day Off

Paco drives away slowly. He drives out into the country. The cotton fields are turning green. Wildflowers are growing along the road. He is thinking hard.

It is Saturday morning, his day off. His day to do whatever he wants to do. He thinks of going fishing. He thinks of visiting his friends from work.

"I'm free now," he says out loud. "I'm my own man." He waits to feel happy. But the ache is still heavy in his chest.

I have my freedom, Paco says to himself. But what have I lost? He thinks of Ramona. She never feels sorry for herself. Or does she? He thinks of the kids and the noise and the mess. How can she stand it?

Paco hears Sal's voice in his head, "Ramona needs some quiet time, too."

Then Paco knows what he has to do. He is going to give Ramona a day off. Today. He will stay with the kids. Ramona can do whatever she wants to do.

As he drives, Paco thinks about it. It sounds good to him. He'll play with the kids. Maybe he'll take them to the park.

Paco thinks of Ramona laughing at him. That makes him smile now. Sal was right. He married a good woman.

Paco turns the truck around and starts for home. But first he stops and pulls over to the side of the road. He jumps out.

Paco picks a bunch of wild flowers. He lays them on the seat. He has not taken flowers to Ramona since before they were married.

Paco gets in and starts to drive away. His heart feels light. He smiles and yawns.

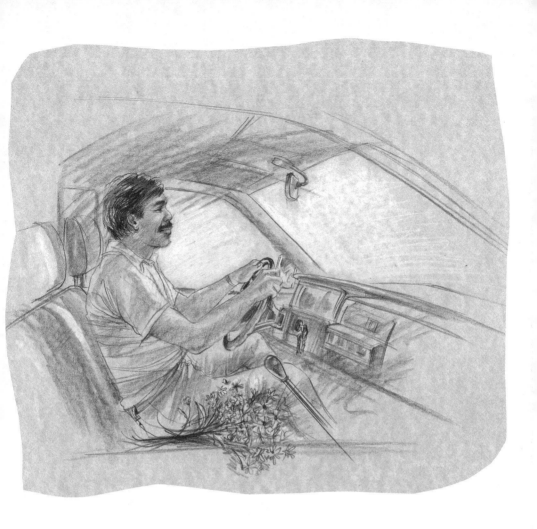

Then Paco thinks of something else. He stops and goes back. He jumps out again and picks another bunch of flowers.

Paco drives back to the diner and runs in. Sal is still there. There are a few customers sitting at the counter.

Paco walks up to Sal. He gives her the flowers.

Sal looks surprised. "What are these for?" she asks.

"Thanks," Paco says. "Thanks for everything." He smiles at Sal and leaves.

Paco drives home. He knows he has once again lost his freedom. He speeds up a little. But he has gained so much more.

About the Author

Rosanne Keller is a writer who lives in St. Joseph, Minnesota. She has taught English as a second language (ESL) and writing. She has taught classes on how literacy affects people. She also has worked as a flagger on a road construction crew.

Ms. Keller makes sculpture and loves to travel. She often writes about the places she visits. Her articles and stories have appeared in many publications. New Readers Press has published several books written by Ms. Keller for ESL learners and adult new readers.

In this book's companion volume, *The Kite Flyer and Other Stories,* you can read four more stories about people with some very human problems to solve. Read-along tapes are available to add another level of learning and enjoyment.